The Very SNEEZY Garbage Truck

By
Marc Schmatjen

Illustrated By
Karina Luong

For my three garbage truck-loving monkeys

— M.S.

For my parents, who helped guide me on my route

even when the going got tough

— K.L.

Bobby the Garbage Truck was a very happy truck.

He had a good job driving around Biggsville, picking up people's trash for them and taking it to the dump.

He liked his job and he was very good at it.

He also had two very good friends, Willy the Street Sweeper and Sam the Fire Engine.

They all lived next to each other on Finkelstein Avenue.

One day, Bobby got a new customer.

The brand new Biggsville Pepper Factory was open for business. They made the pepper for people's pepper shakers.

The new factory had just been built next to the old Biggsville Salt Factory. They made the salt for people's salt shakers.

It was down the road from the Biggsville Shaker Factory. They made the shakers that hold the salt and pepper.

Bobby had just finished picking up the trash at all three factories, and he was driving to his next customer when all of a sudden his nose felt funny.

It itched and it twitched.

And then it tickled and it sniffled.

And then Bobby...

AH-AH-CHOOOOOOO!

SNEEZED!

Bobby sneezed so hard his air horn blew!

HONNNNNNNNNNK!

He sneezed so hard he blew trash right out of the top of his compactor, and right out of the front of his grill.

He made quite a mess, and he was very surprised. Bobby had never ever sneezed before.

Bobby didn't know what to make of his sneeze, but he had a route to finish, so off he went to his next stop.

He was headed into town to pick up the garbage at Peterson's Hardware Store when he saw his friend Willy the Street Sweeper.

He tried to say hello to Willy, but when he opened his mouth, all that came out was, "AH-AH-AH-

CHOOOOOOOOOOO!!!!"

Bobby sneezed again, sending trash flying again, and making his air horn blow even louder and longer this time.

HONNNNNNNNNNNNNNNK!

Bobby was surprised and so was Willy.

Willy said, "Bobby, you sneezed! I don't think I've ever seen you sneeze before."

"I don't think I HAVE ever sneezed before today," said Bobby.

"You made quite a mess," said Willy. "Let me help you clean it up."

"Thanks buddy!" said Bobby.

Willy scooted all around Bobby with his brushes turning and his water jets spraying, and he had the mess cleaned up in no time.

Then Bobby told Willy all about his first sneeze, and they both agreed that Willy should go with Bobby on the rest of his route just in case he sneezed any more.

That turned out to be a good idea, because Bobby kept on sneezing the rest of the day, and every time he did, he would send dust and trash flying in every direction.

And every time Bobby sneezed, Willy would sweep up the mess.

They made a good team.

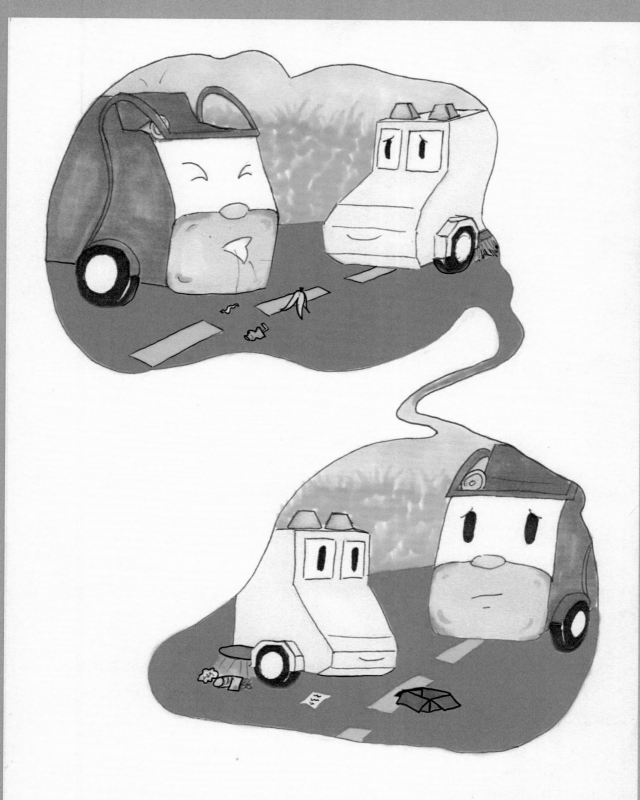

When Bobby was all done with his route, the two friends drove back home to Finkelstein Avenue.

Sam the Fire Engine was there waiting for them, and when he saw them he laughed out loud.

Bobby and Willy were covered in dust from their roofs to their tires from all of Bobby's sneezing and all of Willy's sweeping.

Sam offered to hose them off with his big fire hose, and they both said, "Yes, please!"

As soon as Sam was done washing all the dust off of Bobby, Bobby's nose stopped itching and twitching.

It also stopped tickling and sniffling.

Bobby said, "Sam, I think you cured my sneezing!"

"Have you been sneezing?" Sam asked.

"Yes, all day long," said Bobby. Then he and Willy told Sam all about their day.

After they had finished their story, Sam thought for a while and then said, "I think Willy and I should come with you on your route tomorrow."

They all agreed that it would be a good idea. Then the three friends said goodnight and went to bed.

The next morning the three friends woke up early and got right to work on Bobby's route.

They started at the Biggsville Pizza Parlor. Bobby didn't sneeze after he picked up their trash.

Then they went to Thompson's Auto Parts. Bobby didn't sneeze after he picked up their trash.

He also didn't sneeze after he picked up the trash at the Biggsville Movie Theater, the Biggsville Supermarket, John's Sporting Goods, or Biggsville City Hall.

Then the three friends drove out to where the old salt factory and the new pepper factory and the shaker factory were.

As soon as Bobby was done picking up the trash at the three factories his nose began to feel funny again.

It itched and it twitched.

And then it tickled and it sniffled.

And then Bobby…

AH-AH-CHOOOOOOO!

SNEEZED!

HONNNNNNNNNNK!

"Hmm," said Sam, thinking to himself.

Just like the day before, Willy helped Bobby clean up his mess.

When Willy was finished sweeping up, they all went off to Peterson's Hardware Store. Halfway there, Bobby sneezed again.

AH-AH-CHOOOOOOOOOO!

HONNNNNNNNNNNNNNNNK!

"Bobby, I have an idea," Sam said. "Since you think I cured your sneezing yesterday when I hosed you down, why don't I hose you down again right now?"

Bobby and Willy agreed that it sounded like a good idea, so Sam sprayed Bobby with his big fire hose, and washed all the dust off of him.

As soon as Sam was done, Bobby's nose stopped itching and twitching.

It also stopped tickling and sniffling.

Bobby said, "Sam, I think you cured my sneezing again!"

Sure enough, Bobby didn't sneeze again for the rest of his route and for the rest of the day.

Later that evening when the three friends were back on Finkelstein Avenue, they talked about what had happened.

"I started sneezing at the same place today as I did yesterday," said Bobby. "On my way to Peterson's Hardware Store. After the factories."

"Hmm," said Willy. "After the factories, both times. But you never sneezed after the factories before."

"Nope," said Bobby. "Never."

"How long have you been picking up the trash at the factories?" asked Sam.

"For as long as I've been doing my route," said Bobby. "Except for the new Biggsville Pepper Factory. Yesterday was my first pick-up there. The factory just opened."

"And yesterday was also the first time you sneezed," said Sam.

The three friends thought for a while and then Sam said, "I think the trash at the new pepper factory is making you sneeze, Bobby. I think your nose is allergic to pepper."

"I think you're right, Sam," said Willy. "Since the first time Bobby sneezed was also the first time he picked up the new pepper factory's trash."

"And when you washed the dust off me with your fire hose, you must have washed the pepper right out of my nose!" said Bobby.

"Hooray!" shouted the three friends. "We figured it out!"

So every day after that, Sam the Fire Engine would meet Bobby at the new Biggsville Pepper Factory during Bobby's route.

And every day right after Bobby picked up the factory's trash, Sam would wash him down with his big fire hose, and wash all the pepper right out of his nose.

So that Bobby would never ever sneeze aga... AH...

AH-AH-CHOOOOOOO!

HONNNNNNNNNNK!

Well... not as much, anyway.

The end.

Made in the USA
San Bernardino, CA
24 October 2017